DISPATCHES FROM THE WAR

Peter Cawdron

thinkingscifi.wordpress.com

ISBN: 9798495582842

Imprint: Independently published

"If aliens exist and ever visit us, I think the result will look similar to the first visit of Christopher Columbus to America, which was not so good for the natives."

Stephen Hawking

INTRODUCTION

Dispatches from the War is a series of short stories set in the fictional world of the novel *Welcome to the Occupied States of America.*

These four short stories were developed as promotional material to support the development of the novel as a film by StormLight Media.

Extraterrestrial seedpods have landed in the northern hemisphere. The creatures that have emerged are composite beings. They're capable of disassembling and rearranging themselves to mimic their environment. The world is divided into occupied and free states as humanity battles an invasive species from the stars.

FLOWERS
FOR A
FUNERAL

A light rain falls.

Autumn leaves shuffle across the ground, blown to one side by the wind. Flickers of yellow, red, and orange hide the mud and sludge on the track leading to the farm.

Gravel crunches softly beneath combat boots. Soldiers move in single file. Gloved fingers are substituted for words. Short, sharp hand signals direct the approach along the hedgerow. The squad takes up various positions on either side of a closed wooden door on an old stone building.

Once, soldiers fought for their country. Now, they fight for humanity as a whole. On the right shoulder of each soldier, there's a circular badge with the image of Earth as seen from above the North Pole. The caption under the badge reads, United Nations Reaction Force. Beneath that, their respective flags and an embroidered name are proudly displayed: United Kingdom, France, Germany, Benin, Egypt, Nigeria, and Gabon.

The soldiers are nervous. With their backs pressed hard against the crumbling wall, they prepare themselves for an enemy unlike anything ever seen on Earth.

3

"Keep your eyes peeled for mimics," the sergeant whispers through a throat mic wrapping around his neck. "Duplicates. Identify, but don't touch. Do not engage."

"Copy that," Crosby says. He's on point for the evacuation. He shoulders his M4 and draws a pistol, holding it up near his face. The barrel points at the dark grey sky. He's nervous. His hands are shaking.

"Go," the sergeant says, backing up beside a horse-drawn cart and taking cover. He's expecting the worst.

Without moving from where he is beside the house, Crosby reaches out and wraps his knuckles in the middle of the door. In a firm voice, he calls out, "UN Evacuation Team. Is anybody in there?"

There's no answer.

"UN Evacuation Team. We have confirmation of active heat signatures inside. We're here for your safety. You must evacuate!"

The soldiers wait, but only Crosby and the sergeant are watching the door. The other squad members have fanned out, checking the various approaches to the farmhouse on the edge of the bombed-out village. One of the soldiers crouches on a padded knee, peering through the scope on his M4, looking further along the track. Another has slipped around the corner, watching for anything approaching them across the muddy fields. The others have taken up covering-fire positions near the road. Rifle barrels bristle outward like the quills of a porcupine.

The sergeant nods.

Crosby tries the door handle. Unlocked. He swings the door open and pivots with his gun out, pointing the way. He checks both directions, whispering into his throat mic.

"Left: Coat rack. Red jacket. Small. For a child. Scarf on the shelf.

"Right: Gumboots. Three pair. Identical."

The sergeant replies, "Copy that."

The power is off inside the house. A targeting flashlight set beneath the barrel of his gun provides Crosby with a beam of clarity in the gloomy half-light. His heart races as he steps into the stone house. Outside, the rest of the squad listens in silence.

Crosby creeps down the hallway. Floorboards creak beneath his boots.

The sergeant comes up behind him, following him inside. Unlike Crosby, he's opted for his M4 in the close-quarter confines of the old stone building.

"UN Evac Team," Crosby says, continuing to make his presence known.

Sweat breaks out on his brow in the cold. Moving on instinct, he scans each item down the barrel of his pistol, talking the team through what he sees. A thin beam of light dances over various items as he catalogs possible threats.

"Kitchen: Dog bowl on the floor. One, two, three of them. Only one has food. The others are empty. On the bench, two chopping boards. One clean. There's a large stack of plates beside the fridge. Kettles. Three. Identical. Only one with a power cord."

"Copy that," the sergeant whispers, coming up behind him. "Sanders, get on the horn. Let Archangel know we have an active nest. I need confirmation on the infrared heat count for this place. Is that bird still in the air?"

Crosby creeps on, walking slowly through the old house.

"Dining room: I make eleven chairs jammed in here. The table's in the corner. It's pressed hard against the wall and the window. At best, it would fit three or four chairs."

To get past, Crosby has to shuffle sideways, pressing his back against the wall. He draws his stomach in, making sure he's not going to touch any of the chairs as he moves toward the rear of the house. He keeps one gloved hand on the barrel of the M4 slung over his shoulder so it doesn't bump any of the chair backs.

On reaching the hallway, Crosby turns. The sergeant is no

longer behind him. He's still in the kitchen, paralyzed with fear, looking at all the goddamn chairs. The sergeant's heavy-set, being bigger and more muscular than Crosby. With all his equipment, there's no way he'd make it through the gap between the chairs and the wall.

"I can't do this," the sergeant says. He holds out his hand. His fingers are shaking like leaves in a storm. "Pull back."

Crosby crouches in the far hall, taking a good look at the chairs between them. Outside, the sun is low in the sky. It's broken through the clouds, casting long shadows over the countryside. Sunlight comes in through the windows, catching the chair backs. The wood glistens as though it's been polished with oil. A rainbow-like sheen reflects off all but the three chairs pushed into the table. The sunlight seems to ripple before him. The effect is subtle, like watching waves of heat rising off a concrete road on a hot day.

Over the headset, Sanders says, "Archangel reports the infrared imagery is twelve minutes old. Two survivors. They could see us coming down the track toward them."

"We do not have survivors. Repeat. No survivors," the sergeant says.

"There are no bodies," Crosby says. "They could still be here—hiding."

"There's been no response," the sergeant replies. "We need to get the fuck out of here while we still can."

"I'm good to continue," Crosby says. "I'll check the bedrooms."

The sergeant looks down at his boots. His lips pull tight. He clenches his jaw, but eventually, he nods.

Crosby uses his handgun to push open the next door.

"Study: Two landscape paintings on the far wall. Identical. Desk by the window. Five fountain pens lying side by side. Identical."

"Stay sharp," the sergeant says, although Crosby needs no prompting on that point.

"I—I—I have a body in here. A skeleton. It's in a chair by the bookcase. The bones. They're green. It's as though moss has grown on them."

"And the chair?" the sergeant asks.

"Two chairs," Crosby replies, composing himself and focusing on his task. "Identical. One with a skeleton."

The sergeant growls, "Don't touch nothing!"

"Copy that," Crosby replies, backing out into the hallway.

The next room is a young girl's bedroom. Pretty pink curtains adorn the window. The door is wide open, allowing him to peer inside without stepping onto the carpet. Crosby is about to rattle off what he sees when Sanders comes over the radio.

"Archangel says we have grubs swarming two miles east. Recommend we pull back to the road."

"Wait," Crosby says, already in front of the next bedroom door. "I hear something."

The sergeant says, "What you're hearing is goddamn grubs stripping someone to the bone. Get out of there! Now!"

Crosby ignores him.

"Bedroom two: Lego scattered on the floor. Too much Lego. Unable to spot duplicates."

"Pull back," the sergeant says. "That's an order!"

Crosby continues inching the door open with his boot.

"Bed. One. Picture book. One. Child. I have a child."

"Jesus," the sergeant says.

Crosby holsters his handgun, turning off the flashlight. "Hey there, little fella. What's your name?"

A boy of four or five stares up at the soldier.

"I'm a friend, okay?" Crosby says. He's aware his appearance must be unsettling. The last thing he wants is for the child to panic and run. "Ah, your folks sent me. Mom and Dad. They said, Hey, Crosby, why don't you go in there and play with the little fella? That's it. Mom and Dad said I should come and play with you. Is that okay?"

Crosby steps over the Lego, taking care with the placement of his boots so he doesn't touch any of the small pieces.

"Mom said you like soldiers. If you come with me, I'll introduce you to my friends. They're soldiers too."

The boy ignores his comments and returns to playing with his toys. He mimics the sound of an engine running, making a broom-broom noise with the rattle of his lips. He's lying on his belly in front of his bed, resting on his elbows with his legs behind him, tapping them against the mattress. He straightens a row of matchbox cars in front of him.

"You like cars?" Crosby asks, holding his gloved hands out and gesturing for the boy to stay still. "Me too."

"Threat assessment," the sergeant says in his ear.

"Lego," Crosby whispers. "The goddamn Legos everywhere. So many identical pieces. Ah, he's playing with a fire engine, an ambulance, a white van, and a Ferrari. A red Ferrari. There are two red Ferraris."

"For God's sake," the sergeant says. "Don't let him touch that Ferrari!"

"Easy," Crosby says, feeling as though he's walking in a minefield. "Listen, little guy. We need to go now. Okay? But we're going to leave the cars behind. Okay?"

Crosby points at the two Ferraris off to the child's left. The boy looks at them and reaches out with his tiny fingers.

"No," Crosby snaps, on the verge of yelling but not wanting to scare the boy. Were the boy to run from the room, he could stand on grubs impersonating his Lego or bump into the chairs in the dining room and—whoosh. It would all be over in a heartbeat. Grubs can strip a cow to the bone in seconds. Crosby's seen them in action. Once. He has no desire to see it again. Not with a human. Not with a child.

The boy rests his hand on the nearest Ferrari.

Crosby holds his breath. His fingers are inches away from the boy's arm.

The boy drags his matchbox cars closer, leaving the duplicate Ferrari alone on the carpet.

Crosby gestures at the lone Ferrari and the boy dips his head. He bites his lip but doesn't say anything. His eyes dart between the strange toy and the soldier. It seems he's curious what Crosby's going to do with it.

"That one," Crosby says, pointing. "We don't touch that one, do we?"

The boy shakes his head.

"Crosby," Sanders says from somewhere outside, coming in too loud over the earpiece. "Archangel says there are three people there. Janette Soulazu and her two children. Josh aged three and Amelia aged seven."

"Copy that," Crosby says. "Does anyone have eyes on Amelia?"

"Negative."

"Come here, Josh," Crosby says, swinging his M4 down from his shoulder and onto the carpet. He leaves it there, abandoning it. He has no doubt there will be two M4s within a few hours, but he can't carry both it and the boy. The chance of bumping into something is too great. Crosby reaches out and lifts Josh onto his hip. The boy clutches his fire engine in one hand and an ambulance in the other.

Crosby steps back into the hallway. It's only now he notices a vase has been knocked over. Water has soaked into the carpet.

"I have cut flowers on the ground."

"Flowers?" the sergeant asks, confused by the comment.

"A couple of roses. A carnation. They've been dropped in a row, forming a trail leading to the side door."

"Copy that," the sergeant says. "Hold until we reposition. Squad—on me. Relocate to the east door."

"Negative. Negative," Sanders replies. "Archangel says we have grubs inbound. They're full size. We've got walkers!"

The sergeant says, "Crosby, pull back. Take cover. We'll wait them out."

Crosby doesn't reply. He can see a young girl outside. She's skipping on the cobblestones between the farmhouse and the barn. Her dress is wet but she doesn't seem to care. She's got a bunch of flowers in her hand, swinging them around as she dances to a tune no one can hear.

"I have eyes on," he says, creeping toward the door with Josh on his hip.

"Stand down," the sergeant says. "We have a walker overhead. That fucker is too close for air support."

Crosby positions himself by the open door, leaning against the jamb.

"Amelia," he says, beckoning for her to come to him.

She stops twirling and looks at the soldier as if she's seen a ghost.

"It's okay," he says, adjusting Josh a little higher on his hip. "I'm a friend. Look. Me and Josh. We're friends. Come. Come here."

A shadow blots out the sun.

Pincer-like feet stab at the sodden ground. They're long and thin, cutting into the soil like steel girders falling from a building.

A wooden cart identical to the one by the main door dissolves. Crosby's never seen grubs on the move before. Normally, they lie in wait to ambush their prey. The wooden planks that make up the sides of the cart melt, oozing toward the cobblestones.

"Quick," he says to Amelia.

The steel rims on the cart wheels look as though they're covered in millions of ants swarming down onto the cobblestones. Another pincer strikes from somewhere out of sight in the sky above them, landing between Amelia and the cart. She turns, seeing it. She's frozen in fear.

The wooden spokes at the heart of the wheels sag under the weight of the cart as it collapses to the mud. It melts as though it were made of wax. Like soldier ants in the jungle, the tiny grubs that once made up the cart rush to the pincer, joining it.

"Please," Crosby says, pleading with her. He's outside on the landing, with one hand clinging to the door frame, not wanting to leave the relative safety of a house infected with deadly mimics. Josh clings to him. He's dropped his toys. His grip tightens on the soldier. He moans, burying his head into Crosby's chest.

"Amelia!" Crosby yells, no longer fearing for his own life.

From where he is, Crosby can't see the body of the walker as it towers over the house. Legs stab at the ground as the spider-like creature positions itself in front of Amelia. Its flesh is pale and grey, like that of a rotting corpse.

A grotesque head lowers. Rain drips from its jaw. Dark, compound eyes stare at the young girl, examining her.

Amelia holds up her flowers. Her shoes slip on the wet cobblestones. She struggles to keep her balance. She's on tiptoes with her right arm outstretched above her.

A pincer approaches from the side. Although it's thick and cumbersome, the fine tip separates, taking the flowers from her. The head of the creature recedes, disappearing above the house. The spider-walker continues on, carrying the flowers in one of its smaller claws, close to its mouth.

Crosby rushes over to Amelia. He crouches beside her on the muddy cobblestones, checking her for injuries. She stands still, watching as the walker steps over the trees of a nearby forest. She's shaking. Crosby rests his arm around her shoulder, comforting her as the walker disappears into the gloom.

HALLOWEEN

It's autumn but it feels like summer.

Swallows dart through the air. Moths flutter between the weeds growing out of the cracked concrete. Three teens sneak across an empty lot behind the local shopping mall.

"Come on. What are you afraid of?" Billy Jones asks, lifting a loose chain-link fence.

Jimmy needs to pee. It's just nerves, but they shouldn't be here.

Soldiers drive past. They're looking for looters, but they don't peer into the shadows down the alley.

Actual army vehicles are rare these days. The British Army is too busy fighting the war in the south. As these soldiers are in a brand new neon blue Land Rover, they're probably UN troops brought in to avoid civil unrest. There have been food riots in Glasgow, Manchester, Luton, and Cardiff. London is on fire—and the horde hasn't even reached there yet.

Rifle barrels protrude from the open windows of the Land Rover. It's practical rather than threatening. There are too many soldiers crammed in the car. They lean their rifles against their knees, pointing them up at the sky. They're laughing, which is a good sign.

Jimmy crouches by the fence. "I really don't like this."

Andy's already on the other side, having crawled through on his belly. Grass stains line his football jersey. He's a proud England supporter. The crest over his heart has three lions and a bunch of red roses inside the outline of a medieval shield.

"They're lying to us," Andy says. He points at the metal fire doors at the back of the mall. "I'm telling you. I've seen it for myself. The government's lying. The shelves ain't empty."

"If you're not coming, hold the fence for me," Billy says to Jimmy. He crouches, trying to avoid lying flat on the dirt, but Jimmy can't pull the loose fence any higher. Billy flops onto the grass and shuffles beneath the wire.

"I ain't getting you nothing," Andy says. "If you're too chicken shit to come, that's your loss."

Jimmy's scrawny. He's tall but thin. His pants hang from his hips, threatening to slide down around his ankles. Reluctantly, he drops to his knees and then onto all fours. Billy sticks his fingers through the fence, holding the wire up as Jimmy crawls through.

"You don't believe all that shit about aliens, do you?" Andy asks him.

"It's all over the TV," Jimmy says, getting to his feet and dusting himself off.

Andy says, "Fucking Independence Day was on TV. That doesn't make it true!"

"So where's Will Smith then?" Billy asks Jimmy, looking up at the deep blue sky and throwing his arms wide. "I don't see him chasing no UFOs."

"It's about control," Andy says as the teens walk down the narrow driveway behind the mall. "It's always been about control. They're lying to us to take away our freedoms. Think about it. We've never seen any life in space. We've used hundreds of telescopes to look for these things and we've seen nothing. And suddenly, they're just here? It don't make no sense. Not to me."

There are two dumpsters in the alley. Jimmy doesn't think too much about them, but one tiny detail catches his eye. The exact same cardboard boxes protrude from beneath the half-closed lids. On thinking about it, that's not entirely unusual. Malls carry a lot of stock and it comes in identical boxes. The placement, though, is curious. Rather than being tossed in, the boxes look as though they've been meticulously placed so they're in the same position in each of the dumpsters.

"Huh," Jimmy says, but he doesn't say anything else. Billy and Andy are grumpy enough already. It does get him to hesitate and look back, though. He can't take his eyes off the dumpsters as he walks past. He's not sure what he expects to happen. Nothing's going to jump out at him, but he feels unsettled.

Three cars have been parked beside the loading dock. Like the dumpsters, they're lined up against the wall, leaving the driveway clear.

"Ford Focus," he mumbles.

"What?" Andy asks. He's almost twenty feet ahead of Jimmy, brandishing a crowbar.

"Doesn't that seem strange to you?" Jimmy asks, pointing at the three cars.

"Does what seem strange?" Billy asks, stopping and turning back toward him.

"Why would someone leave three cars here?"

"For fuck's sake," Andy snaps. "What's wrong with you?"

"B—But?" Jimmy stutters.

"No one left three cars here," Billy says. "Three people left a car each. Duh!"

"You don't buy all that alien horse shit, do you?" Andy asks him, slapping his crowbar back and forth against his open palm like a baseball bat. "A bunch of goddamn aliens didn't fly a bazillion miles through space to impersonate a fucking car!"

15

"But there are three of them," Jimmy says. "They're identical."

"That don't mean nothing," Billy says, "The Ford Focus is the most common car in Britain, while white is the most popular color."

"I wouldn't call it popular," Andy says. "Cheap is a better term."

"But they mimic things," Jimmy says, walking cautiously past the cars.

Andy strolls up to the front car. He has a swagger in his step. He's confident. Too confident.

"So this could be an alien?" he asks.

Andy kicks the bumper.

"Come on, you fucker. Fight me!"

Andy works himself into a rage. He swings his crowbar, striking the hood and leaving a dent. He swings it around and scrapes the sharp end over the metal, tearing away the paint, leaving long gouges on the hood.

"There. Are you happy now?" Andy asks. "Because I ain't."

He continues hitting the car, smashing the front lights and the indicators. Broken glass and plastic shards scatter across the concrete.

"Andy!" Jimmy yells, holding out his hands, trying to get him to stop but not getting too close.

Andy's vicious. He's angry. He strikes the windshield with the crowbar. Cracks splinter away from the point of impact. Finally, he staggers backward, out of breath.

Billy kicks the front hubcap, saying, "Definitely not an alien."

"Not an alien," Jimmy says, reluctantly agreeing.

"Do I need to beat the shit out of all of these cars?" Andy asks, pointing with his crowbar.

Jimmy hangs his head, shaking it softly. Andy's always been hot-headed. Jimmy doesn't want to provoke him any further. He just wants to get in and out as quickly as he can.

"Come on," Billy says, jogging up the stairs to the door beside the loading dock. "Let's get on with this."

Andy uses the crowbar to bend the steel frame around the door, gaining access to the lock. It takes some effort, but he pries the door open.

They walk inside. The lights are off. There are no windows in the storeroom at the back of the supermarket. The only light comes from behind them, spilling in through the door. Even Andy's quiet. What seemed like a good idea out in the alley is looking decidedly dumb as they step into the darkness.

Jimmy turns on the flashlight on his smartphone. Without saying anything, Andy and Billy switch theirs on as well. Their lights are feeble, barely illuminating the area immediately in front of them. Something moves in the shadows, scurrying away from them.

"It's a rat," Andy says. "It's just a rat."

"Look," Billy says. He's wandered to one side and is staring up at a storage rack. Boxes of toilet paper stretch into the distance.

Andy says, "See. I told you the shelves were full."

Jimmy says, "You can't eat toilet paper."

"I'll make you eat toilet paper," Andy says, but he's not serious. He's joking around with him. Billy laughs. Jimmy doesn't.

The three teens creep toward the swinging doors leading into the supermarket. There's a glass window built into each door. It's designed to avoid staff bumping into each other as they enter and exit the warehouse. In the darkness, three tiny flashlights reflect off the glass, giving them no visibility beyond the door.

"Shhh," Billy says, pushing lightly on the heavy door.

Andy whispers, "I didn't say anything."

"I thought I heard something," Billy says.

"Not you too," Andy moans.

Billy inches the door open. The others follow him into the store. They emerge near the dairy products. The refrigerators are off, but they're full of plastic milk bottles, cartons of yogurt, blocks of butter, and bags of cheese.

"Look," Andy says, pointing at a row of chocolate milk.

"Shame there's no electricity," Billy says. "It'll have gone off by now."

"Yeah," Andy says reluctantly, on the verge of grabbing one anyway.

They stay together as they creep down the frozen food aisle toward the front of the store. The freezers have been turned off, but they're full of products.

"Such a waste," Billy says.

"I told you they were lying," Andy says, running the flashlight on his phone over boxes of fish, TV dinners, and pizzas. "Oh, man. Ice cream. They let the ice cream go to waste."

"Bastards," Billy says.

Jimmy is silent, trailing along behind them. He worked as a shelf-stocker over the Christmas and New Year's holidays last year. Even on a rare quiet day, there were always items to restock. He's never seen the shelves so full.

"The Halloween decorations are early," Andy says, reaching the promotions area at the end of the aisle, near the front counter. Plastic pumpkins have fallen from the display. They lie scattered across the floor. Someone's opened the candy. There's a pile almost a foot high in the corner.

"Look, skeletons," Andy says, pointing in the eerie half-light of his flashlight.

Bones lie in the next aisle. It's as though someone's dumped a bunch of fake skeletons on top of each other, only they're not made from lightweight plastic. They look solid.

"They're life-size," Jimmy says, not liking what he sees.

"They're in the aisle with the soda," Billy says, edging past them. He swings his backpack off his shoulder, holding it in front of him as he creeps along in the darkness. His back brushes up against the shelves. Bones shift in front of him. Skulls rock as he nudges them with his legs. The light from his phone casts an eerie glow through the empty ribcage of a skeleton piled on top of the others.

"Shit, someone's coming," Andy says, crouching by the checkout.

The three of them turn off their lights, hiding in the darkness. From further down the aisle, there's a rush of noise. To Jimmy, it sounds as though Billy's opened the cap on a fizzy bottle of soda and he's struggling to get the cap back on.

"Billy," Andy whispers. "Be quiet!"

Out in the mall, there's talking. Several high-powered spotlights illuminate the darkness. Beams of light sweep over the store, darting down the aisles.

"Who's there?" a distinctly African voice calls out. "You should not be in here. It is dangerous."

Jimmy peers through a rack of newspapers and glossy magazines.

Soldiers mill around in the entranceway, but they don't enter the store. An embroidered UN badge is visible on each of their shoulders. Beneath those badges, though, there's a different flag. Jimmy's never been any good at recognizing anything other than the Union Jack and the US Stars and Stripes. The multi-national force is from Benin, Gabon, and Zambia, at least. Jimmy's only heard of one of them before. Namibia. And only because they've got a halfway decent football team.

The African soldiers look nervous. They've got their rifles out, aiming at the shelves.

"Come out," one of them yells. "We won't hurt you. We're here to help."

Under his breath, Andy mumbles, "Fuck 'em."

A spotlight flickers over the aisle beside them. Jimmy's expecting to see soda sprayed over the linoleum, but the bottles are all in place on the shelves. A phone lies on the floor. Steam rises from the pile of skeletons.

Jimmy whispers, "Where's Billy?"

"Fucked off home. Fucking coward," Andy says a little too loud.

One of the soldiers steps through the checkout. Jimmy is blinded by the light.

"They're just kids," he says.

"Please," Jimmy says, getting to his feet with his hands raised. "Don't shoot."

"I'm not going to—"

Before he can finish his sentence, Andy shoves Jimmy in the back, pushing him into the soldier. The two of them collapse to the floor, knocking over a magazine stand. The flashlight bounces down the aisle. The other soldiers rush into the store.

Andy runs into the aisle with the skeletons. He grabs a shelf, swinging the rack over and sending bottles of soda crashing to the floor.

Lights dance over the ceiling, walls, and floor as the soldiers rush to help their fallen comrade. Jimmy's expecting to see Andy sprinting for the warehouse at the back of the store, but he's standing perfectly still. His hand is on the shelf even though it's collapsed into the aisle. His eyes are motionless. His body, though, shimmers in the light. Tiny bugs rush along his arms and up his legs. Within a fraction of a second, they've covered him, hiding his face from view. Jimmy's heart barely beats before

Andy dissolves. Steam rushes from his body, leaving nothing more than a skeleton tumbling to the floor.

"What the?"

Jimmy's sitting on the linoleum, but he's being dragged backward by the soldiers. There's yelling, but it's not frantic. They're shouting to each other about cover fire positions and exits. For Jimmy, it's overwhelming.

Two of the soldiers prop his arms over their shoulders and run with him between them. High-powered spotlights illuminate the other shops within the mall as they sprint the length of the hall toward the main doors. Every store is fully stocked. Clothes hang on racks. Toys are on display behind glass windows. A greengrocer has wooden palettes loaded with lettuce, tomatoes, and onions, but none of it is real.

The soldiers burst out into the parking lot. Jimmy's moving his legs, but his feet are barely touching the ground.

"Are you okay, kid?" one of the soldiers asks, letting him stand on his own.

"I—I'm fine. I'm okay."

Another says, "I'm sorry about your friends. Please. Don't go in there. Tell others. Do not come to the mall. It is a graveyard."

Jimmy nods. His lips tremble.

"Where are you from? Where do you live?" the soldier from Benin asks.

"I—um. I live about a mile from here. Up on Coventry Street."

"Don't worry," the soldier from Nigeria says. "We'll get you home. There are evacuations coming. Soon. Soon. They'll take you further north. You'll be safe there."

Jimmy's in shock. His eyes struggle to adjust to the bright sunlight bathing his body. An empty parking lot stretches out before him. There are only three vehicles. Normally, there are hundreds of cars parked on the vast expanse of concrete.

"I don't understand," he says, at a loss about what happened to his friends.

"The aliens," the soldier from Gabon says, as though that is enough of an explanation. "It will be okay. We will give you a ride home."

The soldier from Benin points at the cars. Three brand new neon blue Land Rovers sit next to each other in the middle of the empty lot.

The soldier turns back to Jimmy, saying, "Perhaps it would be best if you walk."

THE ROCK

Flashes of light cut through the night.

Explosions rock the high school even though the blasts are occurring beyond the tree-line, several miles away.

The soldiers in the makeshift command center within the school run along the main corridor, all except Private First Class Jessica Fallon and Private Luis Martinez. They're in no rush. As far as Jess is concerned, they're transporting unstable dynamite.

Luis walks in front of Jess, shielding her. He's got his arms out, waving away anyone trying to take a shortcut between them.

Jess pushes a stainless steel trolley behind him. Luis clears a path for her, pushing soldiers aside. Her gloved hands grip the rail with the intensity of someone hanging from the edge of a cliff.

Cargo straps from a Chinook helicopter crisscross the trolley, holding a mason jar in place on the steel tray. The jar is oversized. It's the kind used to pickle eggs or for storing arts and crafts decorations. Beneath the screw top lid, a single rock sits at the bottom of the glass. Although it's large, it looks ordinary. It's the kind of rock that might be found wedged into a stone fireplace. The sharp sides are rough and unfinished, leading to a jagged point.

Most of the soldiers ignore Luis and Jess. A few of them

peer at the rock as they rush past. There's a look of disdain in their eyes.

"Out of the way," Luis says. "Coming through."

Jess calls out, "Has anyone seen the colonel?"

"Other side of the gym," someone replies. "He's in the science lab."

"Thanks."

Luis and Jess cross the polished wooden floor within the gymnasium. They walk over the basketball key and beneath a torn net, heading for the far door. A sign over the entrance reads science block.

Soldiers stack supplies at the far end of the gym. The high school is a staging post for forward operations. Crates of air-to-surface missiles for the Apaches have been laid out against the coach's office, blocking the door.

The roller doors on the side of the gym have been raised, giving the army access to the football field. Floodlights illuminate the fake grass. The bleachers are empty. Someone's used a Bradley Fighting Vehicle to pull down the goalposts, leaving them lying crumpled in the end zones. National Guard fuel tankers have rolled in from the road. Their wheels have dug up the AstroTurf. Attack helicopters rise into the night, bristling with armament. Their rotors beat at the air like a swarm of angry hornets. They turn and rush toward the battle.

The two soldiers walk into the corridor leading to the science wing. A guard stands outside one of the biology labs. A hastily written sign beside the door says Command and Control.

"Colonel Davis?" Luis asks the guard.

"Inside," is the abrupt reply.

Jess follows Luis. She gets some side-eye from the guard peering down at the rock in the jar.

"Colonel," Luis says, pushing through the soldiers crowded within the lab, but the colonel's on the far side of the room,

24

looking at a map laid out on the teacher's desk. Portable televisions have been set up at the front of the room. Some of them contain live feeds from the fighting, others offer drone footage from above, outlining the extent of the battlefield. One of the TVs offers a confusing list of assets and metrics that are seemingly meaningless. There's an assumption they're important, but to Jess, they're overwhelming and confusing—and invariably out of date.

The desks within the lab are a hive of activity. Soldiers in fatigues work radios, talking to various units. They're coordinating troops, arranging resupply, and organizing medical evacs where needed.

A major intercepts the two of them. He's seen the rock on the tray. He stops Luis with an outstretched arm. "What are you doing here? What's your unit?"

"Easy 2-2," Luis replies.

"You're supposed to be on the northern flank. Why aren't you with your company?"

"We are the company. We're all that's left."

The major is silent, being taken off guard by that revelation, but to Jess, he's a roadblock. She has blood splatted over her uniform. Dozens of dried spots line her cheeks and neck. It's not her blood, but she's lost too many comrades to let some asshole bump her to the back of the line. She doesn't have time for pleasantries. She steels herself, flexing her arms and arching her back as she presses forward. Jess is happy to flatten the major if it gets the attention of the colonel. The major gets the message, stepping to one side as she pushes through.

"What is going on?" the colonel asks, unimpressed by the interruption. He turns to a captain beside him, saying, "We're running a war here, not a goddamn geology collection. Get them out of here."

"Yes, sir," the captain says, stepping in front of Jess and blocking her path. The colonel's pointing at a map, talking about logistics with another officer. Jess will not be deterred. She aims the trolley to one side. Jess doesn't mean to hit the captain, but the wheels ride up over the captain's boots and back down onto the floor as she pushes hard in toward the colonel. She pins him in the corner of the room. That gets his attention.

The captain reaches for Jess, trying to grab her, but Luis steps between them, cutting him off.

The colonel is a volcano about to erupt. His lips pull tight, while his face is flushed with anger.

"By God, there had better be a good explanation for this."

"We've caught one," Jess says.

"What the hell?" the colonel asks. He pushes the cart away. He doesn't even bother looking down at the mason jar.

"This is what we're up against, sir," Jess says, appealing for reason. She points at the glass jar. "This right here."

"I've got four and a half thousand ground troops engaged with air support, fighting a losing battle. I do not have time for your goddamn games."

"Not a game, sir. This fucker took down our platoon."

"That's a fucking rock," he says, marching up to her and staring down at her with unbridled anger. "That," he points at the drop-shot from a drone on a nearby screen. "That's what we're fighting."

Explosions rock the back of a spider-walker towering over trees and homes. The creature steps over parked cars and street signs. An M1 Abrams tank turns the corner. The turret twists. The vehicle rocks as a round is fired, destroying the spider-walker. The creature falls to its knees, collapsing on the road.

Jess refuses to be intimidated. "With all due respect, sir. You do not know what you're up against."

Luis releases the straps. Jess lifts the mason jar with the care she'd give a live bomb.

"Watch," she says, placing it on a ledge at the front of the classroom. She grabs a microscope from a collection of at least twenty others stored on a shelf running beneath the whiteboard. Jess places it next to the mason jar and steps back.

"You are wasting my goddamn—"

The colonel never finishes his sentence.

Within the jar, there's a shimmer of light. A rainbow of colors rolls across the rock. For a moment, it's as though it's a precious stone on display in a jewelry store. He blinks and he's looking at a black microscope within a mason jar.

"Un—fucking—believable," he says, crouching and taking a good look at the newly formed microscope. The eyepiece appears to be made from shiny chrome, while a thin glass plate sits beneath three lenses on an adjustable viewing platform. The base includes a light switch and a knob for altering the magnification.

"That's a—That's a..."

"An alien, sir," Jess says. "A shape-shifting alien."

"And it's safe in there?" the colonel asks.

"No sir," Jess replies. "It could break out of there in a heartbeat."

That gets everyone to step back.

Luis says, "Best we understand it, the damn thing doesn't realize it's in a jar. It's waiting for someone to touch it."

"Like a landmine?" the colonel asks.

"Yes, sir," Luis replies.

Jess points at the nearest TV. She taps on the image of the crumpled body of the spider-walker that's collapsed on the road. The tank has moved further down the street, looking to engage other targets.

"See this?" she says. "It ain't dead. Oh, it looks like it. That shell killed some of it, but not the whole thing. It punched through it without destroying it. Look at the limbs. Look at the way it's fallen against the cars. It's smaller now."

"Smaller?" the colonel asks.

Jess runs her hand over the screen. "Look at how it appears to be melting. It's still alive. It's turning into these things. Send a squad down there to clean up and they're going to get wiped out. They're going to run into hundreds of mimics like this thing in the jar."

She points back at the microscope and the room falls silent.

The major whispers, "Nobody move."

There are three microscopes on the ledge—one on either side of the mason jar. Beneath them, on the storage shelf, another microscope has appeared, replacing the one Jess picked up.

The colonel signals with his hand, waving for everyone to leave. He uses two fingers to point at the door.

The captain turns to the soldiers at the desks, whispering, "Don't take anything you didn't bring in here."

Around the room, soldiers get to their feet and make their way toward the door. Someone at the back of the room moves a chair blocking his path. His clothing bursts into flames. He doesn't even have time to scream. His body convulses as he grips the chair back. Steam rises from his head as his skin dissolves. Within seconds, his skeleton collapses onto the floor. Newly formed mimics create another, identical chair on the other side of his smoldering remains.

Nobody misses it, but nobody panics. They move carefully toward the exit, raising their hands above their heads to avoid bumping anything.

Jess points. There's now a fourth television over by the door. It's off. The screen is black but it's on an identical stand. The colonel nods.

"Leave your gear," he says to the remaining officers and soldiers.

Laptops suddenly appear on the desks, mimicking those that were there moments ago.

The command group edges out of the lab and into the hallway.

Screams echo down the corridor, coming from the gym.

"Get the word out," the colonel says to the captain. "Contact command and tell them what we're dealing with down here. I want intel issued to company commanders, platoons, and squads. We've got to warn our troops about these things."

"Understood," the captain says.

"Issue a general withdraw. Tell command we've been overrun, but not by spider-walkers. And you two," he says, pointing at Jess and Luis. "You're coming with me."

The colonel jogs down the corridor toward the school parking lot. Jess and Luis follow him outside, relieved to have escaped the lab.

Helicopters roar overhead. Tanks maneuver on the main road. Their treads tear up the concrete. The smell of diesel hangs in the air.

The colonel runs for the nearest armored personnel carrier. The ramp is down. He jumps up, grabbing the edge of the vehicle and pulling himself inside. The captain follows him, carrying a large, heavy-duty radio.

Jess comes to a halt.

"No," she yells, seeing there are no lights within the darkened interior. The colonel pauses, turning back toward her and holding out his hand, gesturing for her to join him.

"Run!" she yells, falling to her knees in the parking lot.

The colonel's confused.

It's too late.

The ramp rises, transforming from a drab olive steel tray into a ghostly white, fleshy lip. The treads on the carrier dissolve while the armored panels flex, turning into the pale body of a spider-walker. Legs extend from beneath the creature as it rises into the air. The last Jess sees of the colonel is the bones of his hand hanging from the creature's mouth.

She sits on folded legs, sobbing as the monster rises over the school, walking toward troops gathering on the football field. The bleachers come to life. They coagulate, forming another walker. Skeletons pile up in the end zone, having been discarded by the aliens as they feed.

Luis reaches out his hand, saying, "Come. We've got to make it out of here. We've got to tell command. They need to know what they're dealing with."

The two of them run down the road, disappearing into the darkness, leaving the screaming behind them.

THE WHITE HOUSE

"Grubs have crossed the Potomac," a BBC reporter says, standing on the lawn outside the White House. His accent is out of place in America and yet the gravitas in his voice is apparent. He stands squarely in front of the camera, trying to look calm, but he can't hide the way his body reacts to the thunder unleashed by distant explosions. He may want to be professional and hold still, but his instinctive desire for self-preservation sends a quiver through the muscles in his jaw. Beneath him, the ground trembles.

"Even with a fire-break established along the I-495 beltway, effectively cutting the city in half, the alien menace continues its advance. As you can hear, most of the fighting is on the other side of the river. The 101st Cavalry along with two battalions from the 37th Armor Regiment are engaged in Arlington. The problem is—there's no front line. Not any more. We're getting reports of mimic incursions from Georgetown, on this side of the river, just a few miles northwest of here."

A flight of six Apache helicopters races low overhead. Missiles are launched. Smoke trails rush into the distance, disappearing over the tree line in the park. Buildings crumble as explosions rock the city. Mushroom clouds billow into the sky. They're not nuclear, but they're unleashing hell nonetheless. The incessant thud of rotor blades drowns out the reporter's voice. He yells, wanting to be heard over the roar of the engines.

"The battle is all but over. Washington has fallen. Once the aliens made it to the outskirts of the city, all hope was lost. Their ability to infiltrate within built-up areas makes them impossible to contain. Now they've crossed the river, it's only a matter of time."

He turns, signaling with his hand and pointing at the iconic portico of the White House.

"But this is not just another building. This is a symbol of American power and prestige. Over 250 years of American exceptionalism and democracy is embodied in those walls."

The reporter crouches, wincing as the battle draws closer. He has one hand up by his head, covering his tiny radio earpiece. He's desperate to hear himself, let alone any instructions from his producer. He shouts into the microphone.

"In practice, the White House has already been evacuated. The President is addressing the nation from a secure location on the outskirts of the Capitol. For hundreds of millions of Americans, though, the prospect of losing the White House is unthinkable. When the fighting is in cornfields or on freeways, the alien advance seems abstract. Here, there is no doubt. All talk of containment is meaningless as the grubs close in on this hallowed ground."

Soldiers rush behind the reporter, rolling out concertina razor-barbed wire to form a perimeter on the lawn. There's yelling, but it's not in English. The only words that make any sense are the occasional command issued in triplicate.

"Move! Move! Move!"

A convoy of UN vehicles pulls up on the curved driveway in front of the White House. Chinese soldiers scramble out of the open backs. They're disciplined and aggressive. They set up wooden barricades behind the wire. Within minutes, the pristine green lawn takes on the appearance of a war zone. Chainsaws startup. Steel teeth bite into tree trunks. Sawdust sprays across the grass. Trees fall, crashing on the lawn and digging up clods of dirt.

"Nowhere is the UN presence more keenly felt than here in Washington," the reporter says. "With US casualties approaching two hundred thousand troops in the Blue Ridge theater alone, logistics and support have been turned over to the United Nations. The President said their role would be secondary, but the Chinese soldiers you can see here are prepared for war."

A Chinese officer marches up behind him, yelling, "Move! You move!" He points to Pennsylvania Avenue. He wants the film crew to relocate outside the gates. "You must leave. Very dangerous."

In the background, a mixture of US, German, Russian and Chinese troops work together to unload sandbags, stacking them behind the newly-erected wooden barrier, well back from the concertina wire. Machine guns are mounted on tripods, resting on the wall of sandbags as the soldiers work in unison with each other.

"No one thought the end would come this quick," the reporter says, trying to ignore the officer.

"You go now," the officer says, ignoring the reporter and herding the film crew out onto the street. Instead of the Stars and Stripes, the flag on his shoulder is one of golden stars on a blood-red background. "Please. It is for your benefit."

A row of Humvees pulls up on Pennsylvania Avenue. US troops stand in the open hatchways, brandishing M50 machine guns mounted on rails. Like the Chinese troops behind them, they're facing Lafayette Square, waiting for the approaching horde. A military jet races in low over the city, screaming down along 16th street on the other side of the park. Bombs fall. Fireballs erupt, consuming the buildings. The shockwave rattles the trees, knocking the reporter to his knees. He staggers back to his feet. His ears are ringing, that's obvious from the way he yells to be heard over the following silence.

"It's not a question of life and death," the BBC reporter calls out. His crew clambers into the back of a waiting pickup. "It's just death! That's all that awaits these troops."

He points. The camera follows his direction. Trees throughout the park tremble, but this isn't the aftermath of the explosion. Leaves fall. A shimmer covers the ground, making it impossible to focus on anything beyond the concrete paths. Statues fall. It's as though the park is coming to life. Someone on the pickup drags the reporter by his collar, hauling him onto the bed of the pickup. He stands, holding onto a rail behind the cab.

"Countries are meaningless," he says, determined to report to the bitter end. Around him, soldiers ready themselves for battle. "For once, the world is united. Lines on a map no longer hold any meaning, only the blood, sweat, and tears of the man or woman next to you in the line. These soldiers came here because they're fighting for something greater than themselves. The White House has become a symbol of freedom for the entire world. Should it fall, what hope is there for London, Moscow, Berlin or Beijing?"

One of the film crew slaps his hand on the roof of the cab and the pickup accelerates sharply, bouncing off the curb and onto the road behind the line of Humvees. Soldiers are running everywhere. The camera catches the bitter determination on the faces of those who are about to die.

"Is this it? Is this where we turn the tide?" the reporter asks as the pickup swings onto 17th street. "Or is this the beginning of the end for humanity?"

Tires scream as the pickup slides around the corner. The reporter braces against the back of the cabin. He's struggling not to be thrown out onto the street. Someone grabs his waist, holding him within the pickup.

Gunfire erupts. Clouds of smoke billow into the air. The White House is hidden from view behind the buildings stretching along 17th, but a dark figure rises in the air. Explosions rock the back of an enormous alien creature rising out of the park. Rather than approaching above ground, it has swarmed beneath the city. Now, it looms over the buildings. Alien legs stab at the ground. And then, without warning, the footage is cut and the camera feed goes dark.

The End of the Beginning

AFTERWORD

Thank you for taking the time to read *Dispatches from the War*.

These short stories were developed to highlight the challenges posed in the First Contact novel *Welcome to the Occupied States of America*.

If you're a fan of Philip K. Dick and H.G. Wells, I hope you enjoyed the depiction of the grubs in this novel as a homage to both *The Colony* and *War of the Worlds*. Another influence on this story is the independent movie *Monsters* by Gareth Edwards.

Peter Cawdron
Brisbane, Australia

Printed in Great Britain
by Amazon